Showtime!

For my wife, Lucy Curtin, who helped draft these stories
inspired by the animals of her own childhood.

First published in 2009
by Wayland

This paperback edition published in 2010 by Wayland

Wayland
338 Euston Road
London NW1 3BH

Wayland Australia
Level 17/207 Kent Street
Sydney, NSW 2000

Series Editor: Louise John
Editor: Katie Powell
Cover design: Paul Cherrill
Design: D.R.ink
Consultant: Shirley Bickler

A CIP catalogue record for this book is available from the British Library.

ISBN 9780750256827 (hbk)
ISBN 9780750259934 (pbk)

Printed in China

Wayland is a division of Hachette Children's Books,
an Hachette UK Company

www.hachette.co.uk

Showtime!

Written by Peter Bently
Illustrated by Elisabetta Ferrero

WAYLAND

The horses at Starcross Stables were going to a horse show. Tara helped Mum to put Rascal and Plod into the horsebox.

Smokey, the donkey, and Rocket, the sheepdog, were going too.

"What a lot of horses!" said Tara
when they got to the show.
Dad tied Smokey to the horsebox.

"Poor old Smokey," said Tara, giving him some hay to eat. "Don't get lonely. We'll be back soon."

It was fun at the show. Plod and Dad won a prize for making a furrow in the ground.

"Well done, Plod!" said Tara
giving Plod some tasty carrots.
"Your furrow made a lovely
straight line."

Tara rode Rascal in the children's games. First they won a prize for collecting flags.

Then Tara had to jump in a sack, leading Rascal behind her.

"Well done, Tara and Rascal," said Dad. "That's another prize!"

There was even a race for pet dogs. Rocket ran much faster than all the other dogs.

"Rocket's going to win!" cried Mum.

"Good boy!" said Tara, patting
Rocket. "You went as fast as
a rocket!"

"Come on," said Dad. "We've done so well, let's have an ice cream as a treat."

"It's a shame there are no races for donkeys," said Tara. "Smokey is the only one who hasn't got a prize."

There was a long line of people near the ice cream van.

"I hope they're not waiting to buy ice creams!" said Tara.

"I think they're waiting for donkey rides," said Mum. "But I can't see a donkey."

The woman at the donkey rides
was talking on her phone.
She looked unhappy.

"I'm very sorry," she said to the people waiting. "The donkey is sick, so there'll be no donkey rides today."

All the children looked sad. They started to walk away with their mums and dads.

"Wait!" called Tara. "We've got a donkey!"

"Smokey!" said Mum. "What a good idea, Tara."

Tara and Dad went to get Smokey.
Dad untied him from the horsebox.

"I've got a nice job for you," said
Tara, brushing his hair.

Tara led Smokey on the rides.
He loved being patted and stroked
by all the children.

"What a lovely donkey," said the woman. "He's so gentle."

At the end of the day, Tara helped put the animals back in the horsebox. She gave them each a big bucket of hay.

She hung all the prizes on the horsebox for everyone to see.

They were about to leave when
someone called "Stop!" It was the
woman from the donkey rides.

She gave Tara a big pink rosette.
"This is for Smokey," said the
woman. "All the children loved
riding on him!"

"Thank you," Tara said, hanging up Smokey's rosette. "Now everyone is going home with a prize!"

START READING is a series of highly enjoyable books for beginner readers. **The books have been carefully graded to match the Book Bands widely used in schools.** This enables readers to be sure they choose books that match their own reading ability.

Look out for the Band colour on the book in our Start Reading logo.

The Bands are:

Pink Band 1A & 1B

Red Band 2

Yellow Band 3

Blue Band 4

Green Band 5

Orange Band 6

Turquoise Band 7

Purple Band 8

Gold Band 9

START READING books can be read independently or shared with an adult. They promote the enjoyment of reading through satisfying stories supported by fun illustrations.

Peter Bently lives in Devon with his wife, Lucy and a ready-made audience of two children, Theo (9) and Tara (6). Apart from writing, he enjoys walking, going to the beach, meeting up with friends, and having family fun.

Elisabetta Ferrero works in Vercelli, a town in North Italy surrounded by paddy fields. She lives with her husband and two sons, a hunting dog who loves chasing rabbits but never catches them, six Burmese cats and a gold fish who is 11 years old!